ÆSOP'S FABLES

A Classic Collection of Children's Fables

Illustrated by MILO WINTER

bendon®

The Fox and the Grapes

A Fox one day spied a beautiful bunch of ripe grapes hanging from a vine up in the branches of a tree. The grapes seemed ready to burst with sweet juice. The Fox's mouth watered as he gazed longingly at them.

The bunch hung from a high branch, and the Fox had to jump for it. The first time he jumped he missed it by a long way. So he walked off a short distance and took a running leap at it. He fell short once more. Again and again he tried, but each time, he could not reach the grapes.

Now he sat down and looked up at the grapes in disgust.

"What a fool I am," he said. "Here I am wearing myself out to get a bunch of grapes. They are not worth my effort. I am sure they are sour."

And he walked off with his nose in the air.

There are many who belittle what they cannot get.

THE LION AND THE MOUSE

A Lion lay asleep in the forest, with his great head resting on his paws. A little Mouse came along and ran over his nose, which woke the Lion. The angry Lion laid his huge paw on the tiny Mouse and was about to kill him.

"Oh, please," begged the poor Mouse, "if you will let me go, I promise to repay you in some way."

The Lion laughed at the idea that a little Mouse could ever repay him, but he let him go.

It happened shortly after this that the Lion was caught by some hunters, who tied him with strong ropes to the ground. The Mouse, hearing his roar, came and chewed through the rope with his teeth and set him free.

"Was I not right?" said the little Mouse.

Little friends may prove to be great friends.

The Crow and the Pitcher

~~~

In a spell of dry weather, when the Birds could find very little to drink, a thirsty Crow found a pitcher with a little water in it. But the pitcher was high and had a narrow neck. No matter how he tried, the Crow could not reach the water. He felt as if he would die of thirst.

Then an idea came to him. Picking up some small pebbles, he dropped them into the pitcher one by one. With each pebble, the water rose a little higher. The Crow kept dropping in pebbles until at last the water was near enough to the top so that he could drink.

~~~

A good use of wits may help you out.

THE DOG IN THE MANGER

A Dog was asleep in a manger filled with hay. He was awakened by the Cows, who came in tired and hungry from working in the field. The Dog leaped up and would not let the Cows get near the manger. He snarled and snapped at them as if to say, "This is mine!"

The Cattle looked at the Dog in disgust. "How selfish he is!" said one. "He cannot eat the hay, and yet he will not let us eat it."

When the farmer came and saw how the Dog was acting, he took a stick and drove him out.

Why keep and deny to others what you cannot enjoy yourself?

The Tortoise and the Hare

A Hare was making fun of the Tortoise one day for being so slow. "Do you ever get anywhere?" he asked with a laugh.

"Yes," said the Tortoise, "and I get there sooner than you think. I'll run you a race and prove it."

The Hare was amused at the idea of running a race with the Tortoise. He agreed to it just for the fun of it. A Fox was asked to be the judge, and he marked the distance and started the runners off.

The Hare was soon far out of sight. To make the Tortoise feel even more foolish for trying to race a Hare, he lay down to take a nap until the Tortoise had caught up.

The Tortoise meanwhile kept going slowly but steadily. After a time he passed the Hare, sleeping peacefully beside the road. When at last the Hare woke up, the Tortoise was near the goal. The Hare now ran his swiftest, but he could not pass the Tortoise in time.

Slow and steady wins the race.

The Ant and the Dove

A Dove saw an Ant fall into a stream. The poor Ant struggled to move through the water to reach the bank, but all his attempts failed. The Dove felt sorry for the Ant, and she dropped a blade of tall grass close beside it. The Ant was able to grab onto and cling to the blade of grass, and he floated safely to shore.

Soon after, the Ant saw a man getting ready to kill the Dove with a stone. But just as the man cast the stone, the Ant stung him on the heel. The pain caused the man to miss his aim, and the Dove flew to safety.

A kindness is never wasted.

THE TOWN MOUSE AND THE COUNTRY MOUSE

A Town Mouse once visited a cousin who lived in the country. For lunch the Country Mouse served wheat stalks, roots, and acorns, with a dash of cold water for drink. The Town Mouse ate very little, nibbling a little of this and a little of that. She made it very plain that she ate the simple food only to be polite.

After the meal, the friends had a long talk—or rather the Town Mouse talked about her life in the city while the Country Mouse listened. They then went to bed in a cozy nest tucked away in a haybale and slept in quiet and comfort until morning.

In her sleep the Country Mouse dreamed she was a Town

Mouse with all the fancy foods and delights of city life that her cousin had described for her. So the next day when the Town Mouse asked the Country Mouse to go home with her to the city, she gladly said yes.

When they reached the mansion in which the Town Mouse lived, they found on the table in the dining room the leftovers of a very fine banquet. There were jellies, pastries, delicious cheeses—the most tempting foods a Mouse can imagine. But just as the Country Mouse was about to nibble a dainty bit of pastry, she heard a Cat meow loudly and scratch at the door.

In great fear, the Mice scurried to a hiding place, where they lay quite still for a long time. They hardly dared to breathe. When at last they crept back to the feast, the door opened suddenly. In came many servants, followed by the big House Dog.

The Country Mouse stopped in the Town Mouse's den only long enough to pick up her carrying case and umbrella.

"You may have rich foods that I have not," she said as she hurried away, "but I prefer my plain food and simple life in the country with the peace and safety that go with it."

It is better to live simply and safely than to live with riches and fear.

The Ants and the Grasshopper

One bright day in late autumn, a family of Ants was bustling about in the warm sunshine. They were busy drying out all the grain they had stored up during the summer. Along came a starving Grasshopper with his fiddle under his arm. He came up and humbly begged for a bite to eat.

"What!" cried the Ants in surprise. "Haven't you stored anything away for the winter? What in the world were you doing all last summer?"

"Oh, well, I didn't have time to store up any food," said the Grasshopper. "I was busy making music and having fun. Before I knew it, the summer was gone."

The Ants shrugged their shoulders in disgust.

"Making music, were you?" they cried. "Very well—then, now you can

dance!" And they turned their backs on the Grasshopper and
went on with their work.

There's a time for work and a time for play.

Two Stubborn Goats

There were once two Goats who were each walking on opposite rocky sides of a mountain valley. It so happened that a large tree had fallen, forming a bridge between the two sides. Far beneath this bridge there flowed a wild river.

Now, the two Goats each started to cross the bridge and looked up and saw each other. The trunk of the tree was large, but not large enough for one animal to pass another safely. One Goat would have to wait for the other to cross. And do you think one Goat would back up and allow the other to pass? No! These Goats were both too stubborn!

One Goat set his foot on the log. The other did also. Each kept walking until they met in the middle, horn to horn. Neither would back up nor step aside. Instead, they locked

horns and pushed at each other—and both fell, down, down, down into the river below.

It is better to step aside than to stubbornly step into disaster.

THE PEACOCK'S TAIL

The Peacock, they say, did not at first have the beautiful feathers he now has. It seems that there was a time when the Peacock begged Juno, the queen of the gods, for a rich train of feathers grander than any other bird. Juno granted his request. With his new gleaming tail of green, gold, purple, and blue, he strutted around proudly among the other birds. All who saw him envied him, which pleased the vain Peacock greatly.

The Peacock then saw an Eagle soaring high up in the blue sky. "Ah!" said the Peacock. "How amazing I will look when I fly with my new robe of feathers."

Lifting his wings, the Peacock tried to rise from the ground. But the weight of his magnificent train held him down. Never again could he fly up to greet the first rays of the

morning sun or the rosy clouds at sunset. Instead he would
have to walk the ground with his long, heavy tail of beautiful,
royal feathers.

Gain of riches can also bring loss of freedom.

Belling the Cat

The Mice once called a meeting to decide on a plan to free themselves of their enemy, the Cat. They wished to find some way of knowing when she was coming, so they might have time to run away. Indeed, something had to be done, for they lived in constant fear of her claws. The Mice hardly dared to stir from their dens by night or day.

Many plans were discussed, but none of them was thought good enough. At last a very young Mouse got up and said:

"I have a plan that seems simple, but I know it will work. All we have to do is hang a bell about the Cat's neck. When we hear the bell ringing, we will know immediately that our enemy is coming."

All the Mice were surprised that they had not thought of such a plan before. But as they clapped and rejoiced, an old Mouse arose and said:

"I will say that the plan sounds very good. But let me ask one question: Who will bell the Cat?"

It is one thing to say that something should be done, but quite a different matter to do it.

The Fox and the Crow

One bright morning a hungry Fox was following his sharp nose through the forest in search of a bite to eat. He looked up and saw a Crow on a branch of a tree overhead. This was by no means the first Crow the Fox had ever seen. What was different about this Crow was that the lucky Crow held a bit of cheese in her beak.

"No need to search any farther," thought the sly Fox. "Here is a tasty bite for my breakfast."

Up he trotted to the foot of the tree. He looked and smiled, saying, "Good morning to you, beautiful lady!"

The Crow cocked her head to one side and watched the Fox. She did not trust Foxes, so she kept her beak tightly closed on the cheese and did not say good morning.

"What a charming creature you are!" said the Fox. "How your feathers shine! What splendid wings! I'm sure you have a lovely voice, since everything else about you is so perfect. If you would just sing one song, everyone in the forest would call you the Queen of Birds."

The Crow listened to these words and was quite flattered. She forgot all about not trusting a Fox. She forgot about her breakfast. She forgot that she was, after all, a Crow who did not have a lovely voice. All she thought of was how she wanted to be called the Queen of Birds.

So she opened her beak wide to sing. But, of course, instead of a lovely song, out came a loud caw—and down fell the cheese, straight into the Fox's open mouth.

"Thank you," said the Fox sweetly, as he walked off. "I did not enjoy your song, but I will enjoy your cheese."

Beware the one who flatters — he wants more than your smiles.